**Welcome to
The Luniverse.**

ABOUT THE LUNICORN

The Lunicorn

A media brand producing informative and engaging video series that explore and uncover business culture in the global innovation industry.

From startup cities to founder fails, and everything in between, all delivered in quick-bites of infotainment.

Lunicorn Productions

Creative agency and production house focused on creating short-form video content for the innovation industry.

We help the smallest of startups, to the biggest of tech giants tell stories and communicate to a mobile first media consumer.

ABOUT THE BOOK

The Why

Why not?!

The What

A cartoon illustrated startup journey from *idea* to *exit* explained by The Lunicorn. With 23 of the most common terms, any founder should get to know, with a few hidden industry references for good measure. Can you spot them?

The Who

If you have ever been stuck in a WeWork elevator, listening to someone complaining about their *burn rate*, this is the book for you.

Or anyone that just wants a dictionary to help decipher

SCAN THE QR CODE

How to scan a QR code

Every buzzword in this book has an online component. By scanning the QR code in the middle of the right page, you will unlock a video and dive deeper into The Luniverse.

Make sure you have access to the internet. Then open your camera, hover it over the QR code (don't take a picture), a pop-up will appear after a few seconds. Click the link to open a webpage with the video and more.

If you have an older version of Android, you may need to download a QR code reading app… ah, should have followed the *tribe* ;)

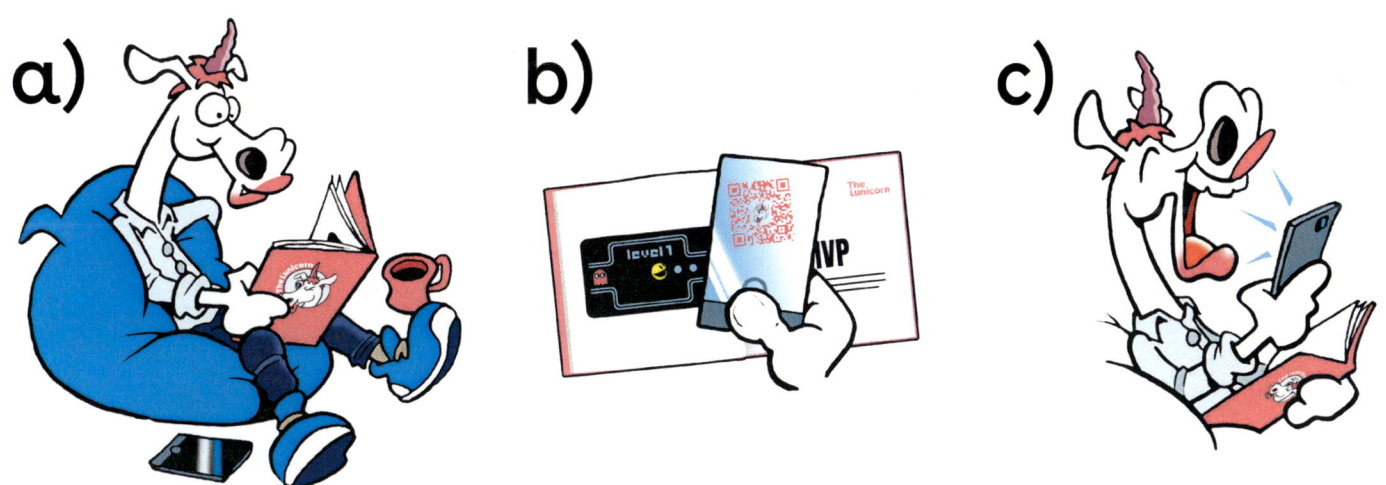

a) b) c)

TABLE OF CONTENTS

Page index

Bootstrapping	11
Stealth Mode	13
MVP	15
Beta Test	17
Pivot	19
Accelerator	21
Hockey Stick	23
Pitch	25
Angel	27
Convertible	29
CoWorking	31
Growth Hacker	33
Traction	35
Tribe	37
Deck	39
VC Money	41
Burn Rate	43
Runway	45
Bridge	47
Scale Up	49
Ramen Profitable	51
Unicorn	53
Exit	55

BOOTSTRAPPING

Funding your startup using your own salary, savings or a side hustle business, like consulting or having a lemonade stand.

The Lunicorn

STEALTH MODE

When founders think their idea is so great that they don't tell anyone about it and work secretly under the radar.

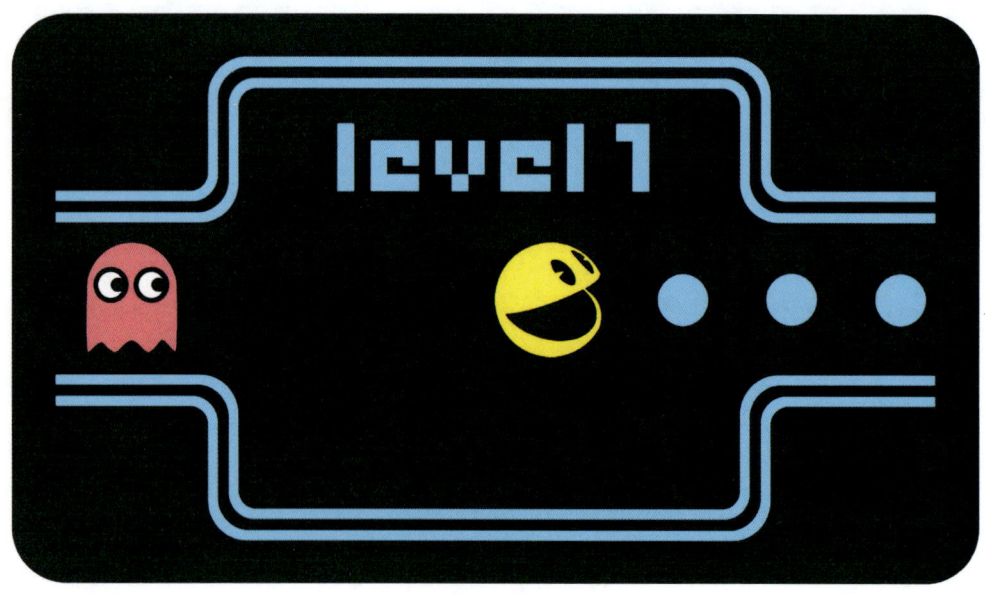

The Lunicorn

MVP

The minimum viable product is the first version of your product, that you use to test with customers to see if there is a product-market fit. And for most, it's very very basic with lots of dead ends.

The Lunicorn

BETA TEST

Testing the MVP with a group of early adopting customers, to learn how they interact with it so you can make changes based on this, or in some cases, go back to

PIVOT

After testing a product, some startups decide to change industry or business model based on this feedback.

ACCELERATOR

A 3 to 6 month program, sort of like a school for founders to get accelerated learning. Finishes with a graduation called a demo day.

HOCKEY STICK

A real startup cliché, forecasting revenues to look like they will go up, up and up.

PITCH

Presenting your startup in only 3-5 minutes in front of an audience, it's like every founder's Pop-Idol moment.

The Lunicorn

ANGEL

An individual who invests in an early-stage startup, and helps with industry knowledge as well as money. They are mostly looking for the right team or The A-Team!

CONVERTIBLE

When it's too hard to value your startup in the early phases, you take a loan from angel investors that converts into shares at a later point.

COWORKING

The natural habitat of the founder, with free coffee, beer on tap, and glass walls; kind of like a startup playhouse.

GROWTH HACKER

Someone who finds ways to speed up processes and growth using creative and sometimes crazy methods.

TRACTION

Business metrics such as visitors to your website, or increasing sales that you show investors to demonstrate that you have momentum or *traction*.

TRIBE

A company or consumer culture that everyone believes in, or buys into religiously, following one another like lemmings, or lemons.

37

The Lunicorn

DECK

Your startup's slide presentation. So, when an investor says "show me your deck" they mean your slides, or cards as we like to think of them.

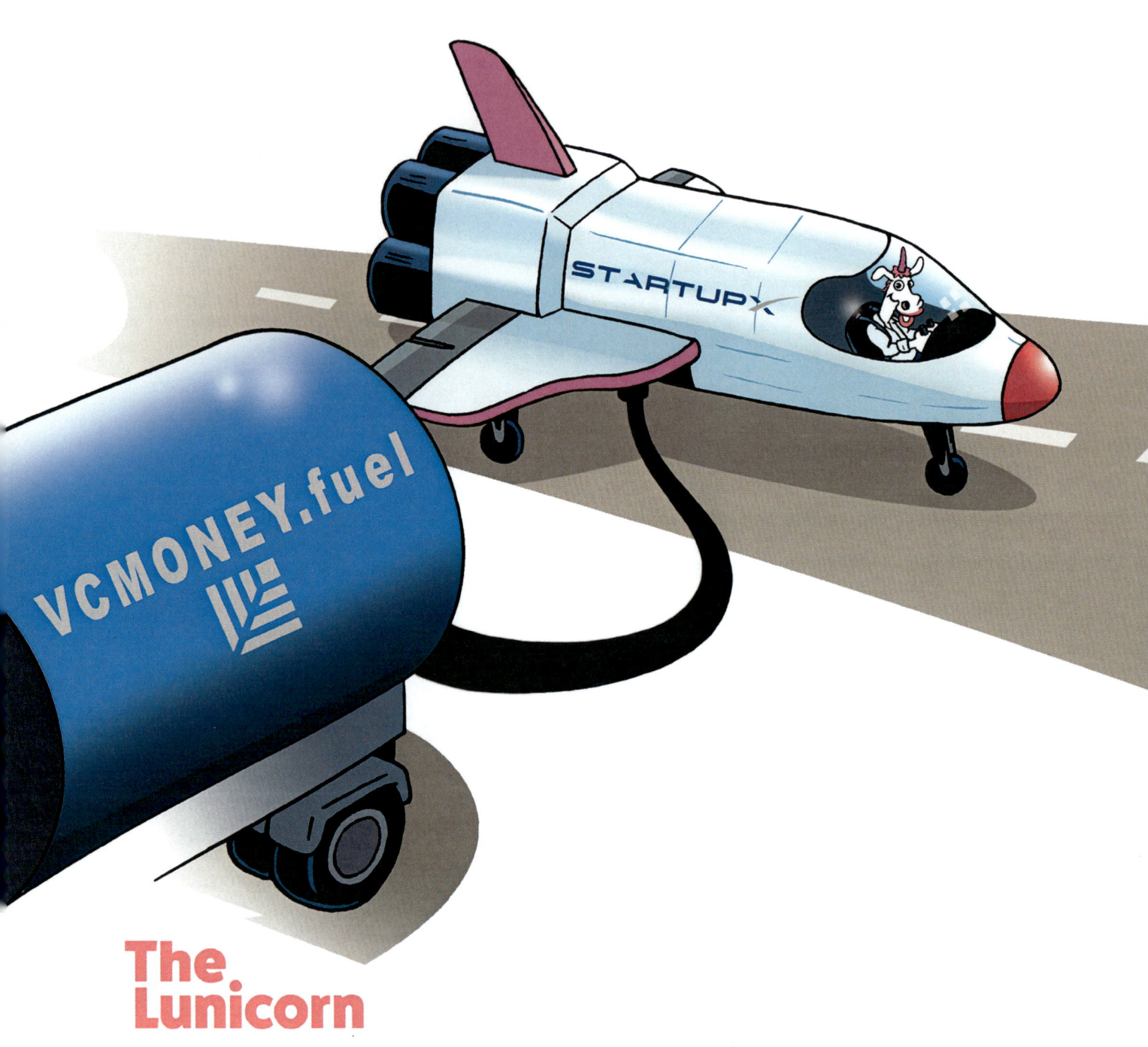

VC MONEY

Venture capital investment is known as rocket fuel, as it comes with help, support, and pressure to deliver.

The Lunicorn

BURN RATE

In the startup world, money equals fuel; your burn rate is the amount of fuel you burn every month.

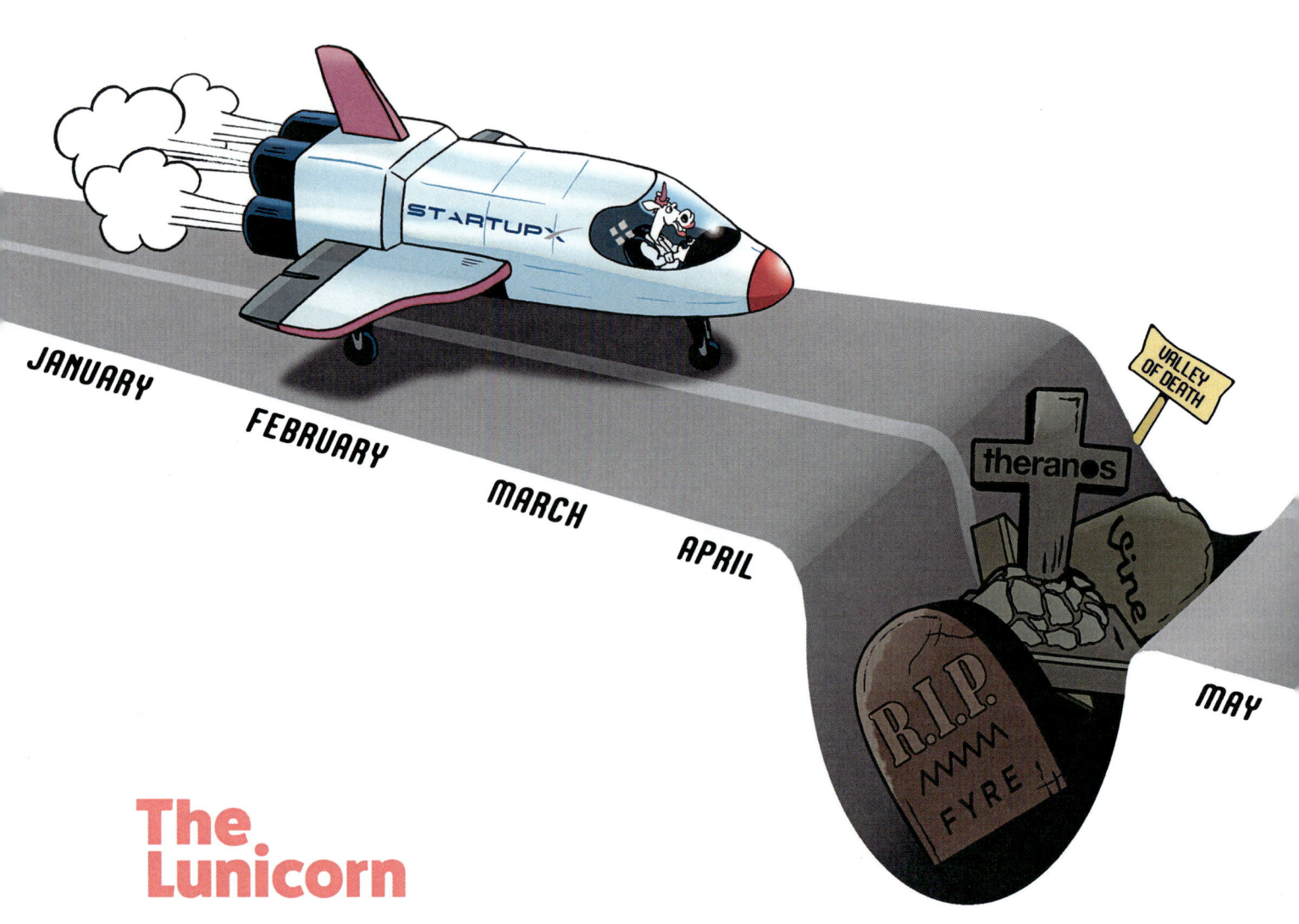

RUNWAY

If your burn rate is $10K per month, and you have $30K in the bank, your runway is 3 months before you plunge into the valley of death.

BRIDGE

A short-term loan of money to bridge the gap between financing rounds ... as funding always takes longer than you think!

SCALE UP

When a startup finds its groove, increases its team, streamlines operations, and becomes a proper business.

RAMEN PROFITABLE

When your startup has just enough profit to afford you a bowl of noodles, but nothing more.

UNICORN

A startup that reaches a $1bn valuation is called a unicorn. It's the thing of dreams for most founders and investors. Usually this means you need to raise a lot of money, standing on the shoulders of your investors.

EXIT

The Holy Grail of the startup journey. An exit means the ability to sell some of, or all of the shares in your compa-

PLAY THE GAME

Congrats, you made it through! But how many buzzwords can you remember? Take the test and see how fluent you are in startup lingo.

ABOUT AUTHOR

As a show host and former VC, I wanted to freshen up the often dry and technically worded formats that most of the startup media use to present topics and themes in the innovation industry.

So I founded The Lunicorn to bring infotainment into the ecosystem.

Ultimately, I want to humanise innovation, and make entrepreneurship available to all.

BIG THANKS

To my team, without whom this book would never have made it to print.

To my investors, who have backed and believed in my team's vision and ideas, no matter how quirky at times.

And to you, my readers. I hope that you have learnt something, and maybe even laughed along the way.

Design & illustration: www.sveen-emberland.com

Made in United States
North Haven, CT
06 September 2023